For any little cheese with
big ooh-la-la dreams —E. P.

For Peter —D. G.

SIMON & SCHUSTER BOOKS FOR YOUNG READERS · An imprint of Simon & Schuster
Children's Publishing Division · 1230 Avenue of the Americas, New York, New York 10020 · Text copyright © 2012 by Elise Primavera ·
Illustrations copyright © 2012 by Diane Goode · All rights reserved, including the right of reproduction in whole or in part in any form.
SIMON & SCHUSTER BOOKS FOR YOUNG READERS is a trademark of Simon & Schuster, Inc. · For information about special discounts for bulk purchases, please
contact Simon & Schuster Special Sales at 1-866-506-1949 or business@simonandschuster.com. · The Simon & Schuster Speakers Bureau can bring
authors to your live event. For more information or to book an event, contact the Simon & Schuster Speakers Bureau at 1-866-248-3049 or visit our website
at www.simonspeakers.com. · Book design by Jessica Handelman · The text for this book is set in Lomba. · The illustrations for this book are rendered
in watercolor. · Manufactured in China · 1111 SCP · 10 9 8 7 6 5 4 3 2 1 · Library of Congress Cataloging-in-Publication Data · Primavera, Elise. ·
Louise the big cheese and the Ooh-la-la Charm School / Elise Primavera ; illustrated by Diane Goode.—1st ed. · p. cm. · "A Paula Wiseman Book." ·
Summary: Louise, who wants nothing more than to be important, jumps at the chance to attend a charm school run by Claire Eclaire, who is from
Paris. · ISBN 978-1-4424-0599-8 (hardcover) · [1. Etiquette—Fiction. 2. Friendship—Fiction.] I. Goode, Diane, ill. II. Title. · PZ7.P9354Ll 2011
· [E]—dc22 · 2009047236 · ISBN 978-1-4424 8257 9 (eBook)

first
edition

LOUISE THE BIG CHEESE

AND THE Ooh-la-la CHARM SCHOOL

Elise Primavera

ILLUSTRATED BY Diane Goode

A PAULA WISEMAN BOOK
SIMON & SCHUSTER BOOKS FOR YOUNG READERS
New York London Toronto Sydney

LOUISE CHEESE was a small girl who lived in a sleepy town on a quiet street in a modest house.

She longed for her mother to invent something important like the marshmallow. She wished her father drove a very important car that could fly.

But Mr. and Mrs. Cheese didn't think it was very important to be very important.

Louise didn't agree. She wanted to be a very important person. In fact, Louise Cheese wanted to be a big VIP.

In Louise's house no one ever noticed her.
No one noticed her even if she put on the Mexican
hat that she wore for her kindergarten dance recital.

Louise put on her Christmas pajama bottoms,
her Halloween T-shirt, and her swimming flippers.
"Hi, Penelope. Notice anything different?"

Outside on Puddle Street, Louise rode her bike around the neighborhood to see if anyone important would notice her.

As usual her best friend, Fern, was in the backyard in her tree house, where she was making something. She called to Louise, but Louise didn't notice.

Louise passed Mrs. Jumbolla, who had the nicest house on Puddle Street;

old Mr. King, whose dog, Buster, could ride a skateboard;

and Miss Goldstar, who once found a turtle the size of a garbage can lid in her backyard.

Not one important person noticed me.

Unbelievable.

Louise was almost all the way around the block.
She wished that, for once, someone would notice her.
"Bonjour!" a voice said.
 A girl was walking across a lawn balancing a book on her head.

"My name is Claire Eclaire. I am visiting my *Grand*-mama, and I am from Paris!"

"Wow," Louise gasped. "What's it like in Paris?"

"Everyone owns a pink poodle," Claire Eclaire replied. "All the girls pile their hair way up on top of their heads in what they call a 'croissant.' And every day they dress in gold ball gowns and eat cupcakes in French bakeries."

Right away Louise knew that Claire Eclaire was the most important person she had ever met.

"I wish I was ooh-la-la," said Louise.

"Come back tomorrow and you can attend my Ooh-la-la Charm School."

When she got home Louise told everyone to take a good look at her because soon she was going to be very ooh-la-la and important, and that she would, most likely, be moving to Paris.

"Don't forget to write. You'll always be our little Louise!" her parents said.

That night Louise dreamed about how everybody would treat her once she got to be ooh-la-la and important.

Louise dreamed that she got invited to go on a ride in a rocket ship to Mars, where there was a very important party that only big VIPs could go to.

At the party everyone went around saying *Bonjour!*

The next morning when Louise woke up, she felt a lot more important than when she went to bed.

And even better, Louise didn't need to straighten up her room. She ate her cereal out of the box, chewing with her mouth open, and she burped out loud with her elbows on the table.

Louise didn't care. She couldn't wait to see Claire Eclaire
and start Ooh-la-la Charm School.

But just as she was about to go, Fern stopped by.

As soon as she got to Claire Eclaire's house, they got right to work.

Louise walked around with a book on her head. . . .

Next Claire Eclaire did Louise's hair.

Then Claire did PeeWee's hair.

After that Louise learned about the proper way to play Candy Land.

The next day Louise learned how to make a bed the way they do in Paris, and put away all Claire's toys— just the way they do in Paris!

As a special treat at the end of the day, Claire Eclaire made Louise an ooh-la-la outfit.

"Tomorrow," Claire said, "is graduation from Ooh-la-la Charm School, but first you will have to take a BIG exam— and it will take place at a French bakery. I will pick you up at nine a.m. sharp!"

French bakery? Louise had never been to a French bakery before.
Would she be ooh-la-la enough to pass the test? On the way back to her
house, Louise worried—but for the first time Louise also got noticed.

Fern called out to her, but Louise didn't hear—
she was rushing home to show everyone
how ooh-la-la she was now.

Good day.

Hello.

Hi.

Hey,
Louise!

When Louise got home,
her mother said hello, her
father waved, and her sister,
Penelope, laughed at her.
Penelope *really* laughed at her.

That night Louise dreamed she was in an important French bakery
with big VIP, ooh-la-la people licking frosting off giant cupcakes,
and pink poodles were laughing at her in French.

Then the dream changed and she saw Fern waiting by the phone.

When Louise woke up, she remembered that she didn't keep her promise to call Fern—her true best friend. Louise never felt so unimportant in her entire life.

But at 9:00 a.m. sharp, Claire Eclaire had different ideas. "I hope you're ready for the BIG exam at the French bakery," she whispered and pinched Louise hard as she got in the car.

"It's so nice that Claire has a friend," Claire Eclaire's mother said as she drove. "No one seems to want to play with her in Maine."

"Paris, Maine," said Mrs. Eclaire.

Instead of a French bakery, they pulled into a gas station.

"But it's so nice you girls got a chance to say good-bye," Claire's mother said.

"Good-bye?" Louise said, and Claire pinched PeeWee hard.

Mrs. Eclaire got gas in the car and drove to Louise's house.

"We're leaving today, but maybe you could visit us in Maine!" she said brightly.

Ooh-la-la Diesel

FREE donut OR cupcake With every full tank!

White-glove service!

Hot $1.00 Coffee

Have a

#1.

BONJOUR GAS STATION

Merci, non!

"Au revoir!" Claire Eclaire called, and stuck her tongue out at Louise as the car sped away.

Louise was relieved to be rid of Claire Eclaire,
and now all she wanted was to find Fern.

She ran down Puddle Street to Fern's house,
but Fern wasn't there.

Next Louise looked in Fern's backyard up in the tree house where Fern was always making something. But Fern wasn't there, either. Louise was afraid Fern wasn't her friend anymore.

PeeWee didn't say anything because he thought Louise might be right.

But Louise was wrong, because Fern suddenly appeared around the corner of her house.

"There you are, Louise!" Fern shouted. "I have something really important to give you!

Wrapped in pink paper was a beautiful charm bracelet. "I made it from a kit," Fern told her.

Louise handed PeeWee to Fern and then climbed up the tree after her. No, it wasn't Paris, France, and they weren't big VIPs, but right then sitting in the tree house on Puddle Street, happy together with Fern and PeeWee, seemed to Louise like the most important place in the world to be.

I still want to be ooh-la-la. Take my quiz and see if you've got what it takes to be a big VIP, ooh-la-la charmer!

1. My new pet is going to be:
   a. a hamster named Freckles.
   b. a goldfish named Fred.
   c. a French poodle named Françoise.

2. At my birthday party, I plan to serve:
   a. hot dogs.
   b. mac and cheese.
   c. giant cupcakes from a French bakery!

3. At the end of the school year, I'm giving my teacher:
   a. a pot holder from the pot holder–making kit my aunt
      gave me on my last birthday.
   b. some leftover Halloween candy.
   c. a trip to Paris.

4. The most ooh-la-la clothes I have are:

   a. my Sunday underpants.

   b. my sister's velvet headband that she gave me after the dog
      chewed it.

   c. my ball gown with a giant red bow.

5. If I want to charm everyone I meet, I:

   a. would hand out cough drops.

   b. would hand out deodorant.

   c. would hand out candy and tell everyone they have good hair.

6. This summer I hope to get a snapshot of myself:

   a. in an Amish dress at a quilting bee.

   b. in overalls in front of a wigwam.

   c. in a gold ball gown in front of the
      Eiffel Tower.